THIS BOOK BELONGS TO

DISCARD

DEPUTY
U.S.
MARSHAL

PUT THE CD ON! TURN THE PAGE!

DEDICATED TO
DREAMERS EVERYWHERE

Published simultaneously in Canada by Thomas Allen & Son Ltd.
Library of Congress Cataloging-in-Publication data is available.
WORKMAN PUBLISHING COMPANY, INC.
225 Varick Street, New York, NY 10014-4381
WORKMAN is a registered trademark of Workman Publishing Co., Inc.
Manufactured in China   First Printing September 2013   10 9 8 7 6 5 4 3 2 1
ISBN 978-0-7611-7176-8

~ Part One ~
Look While You Listen

I've got a dog. He's really smart. Got soulful eyes, and a big ol' heart.

SONG 1

✨I've Got a Dog✨

I've got a dog.
   And he's got me.
We get along
so easily.
Wherever I go,
he's by my side.
I've got a dog.
I'm satisfied.

I've got a dog.
He howls along
whenever I play
a lonesome song.

I've got a dog.
I call him Hank.
My lucky stars
I sure do thank.

Well, he won't win a prize
for being dog-pretty
at a fancy show
in the great big city.
He's a mix of hound
and I-don't-know-what.
A hundred percent
pure Junkyard Mutt.

LEAP TO PAGE 36
FOR MUSIC AND
FULL LYRICS!

Silver trucks and rusty trucks and every truck you see.
As long as it's a truck, well it's just fine by me.

SONG 2

⌇Trucks⌇

I'm sitting in this living room,
just playing my guitar.
And now there comes a rumbling sound
from I don't know how far.
I go right to the window till she comes into view.
There's no one nowhere anyhow loves trucks the way I do.

GET ROLLING—

Big trucks and little trucks and long trucks and tall.
Old trucks and new trucks, delivery or long-haul.
Silver trucks and rusty trucks and every truck you see.
As long as it's a truck,
well it's just fine by me.

LEAP TO PAGE 37 FOR MUSIC AND FULL LYRICS!

SONG
3

FROG TR

CHORUS OF EARNEST COWBOYS:

There's a wind from the West, and it blows mighty restless and free.

ROUBLE

And you know that it's best if you go, for there surely will be TROUBLE. *Ooo-oo…*

★ THE SONG CONTINUES →

There's only one thing gets a Cowboy down.
It's the kind of trouble that we've got in this town—Frog Trouble.

ᘯ Frog Trouble ᘯ

OKAY, STRANGER—

You don't know me, and I don't know you,
but I'm telling you this, and it might be true.
There's only one thing gets a Cowboy down.
It's the kind of trouble that we've got in this town—
Frog Trouble. *Hmm-mm.*

When I'm walking along, minding my own
business, they ought to leave me alone.
If you ask me how I'm doing today, I shake my head.
I've got two words to say: Frog Trouble.
AND HERE'S TWO MORE: Frog Trouble.

Hmm-mm.

LEAP TO PAGE 38
FOR MUSIC AND
FULL LYRICS!

Please let me stay up too late. I don't want to go to bed.
I'm not even tired. I just want to play instead.

SONG 4

❧ Heartache Song ❧

THEY MAKE ME—
clean up my room. And put away my toys.
When company comes, I can't make any noise.
Oo-wuh uh-uh uh-oh!

THEY SAY—
I must take a bath. But I've had one before.
I'm just so upset.
I can't take any more.

DON'T THEY REMEMBER—
all the heartache so deep
when somebody tells you
it's time now for sleep?

LEAP TO PAGE 40 FOR MUSIC AND FULL LYRICS!

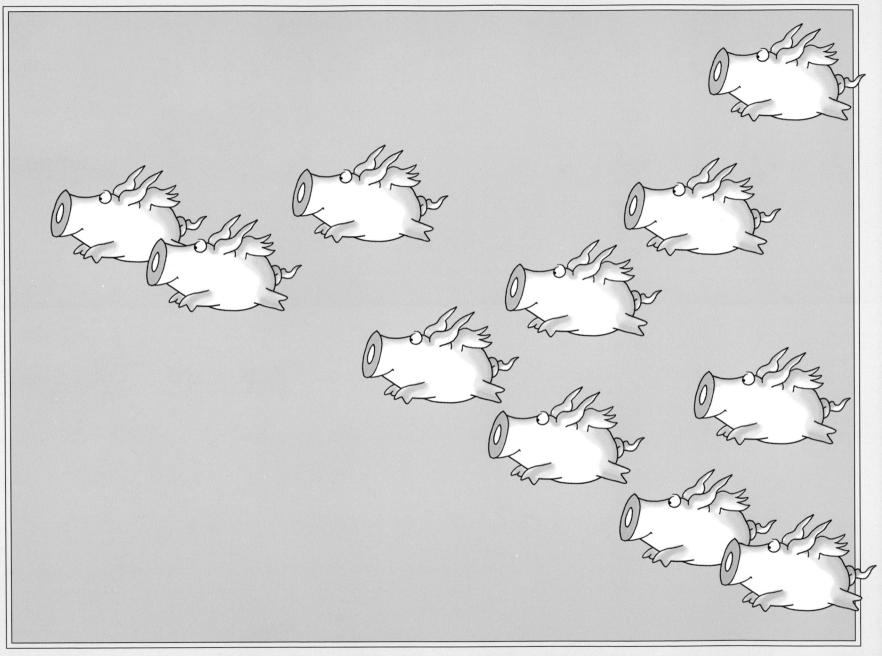

It's a beautiful thing—When Pigs Fly.

SONG 5

ꙮWhen Pigs Flyꙮ

I know you for a dreamer,
'cause I've been a dreamer, too.
You've got that faraway look in your searching eyes,
and a heart that's steady and true.
And I think I know what you're looking for
in the endless blue of the sky.
You wait for the time—When Pigs Fly.

Did I hear somebody tell you
that dreams are nothing but air?
Did I hear somebody try to say
imagination will take you nowhere?
If anyone says it can't be done,
that's the time to simply reply:
"It's a beautiful thing—When Pigs Fly."

LEAP TO PAGE 41 FOR MUSIC AND FULL LYRICS!

My Granddad listened to me play, and he began to smile.
He played a fiddle tune for me. We both played for a while.

SONG 6

❧ Broken Piano ☙

I don't know just how old I was, but when I was quite small,
I found an old piano that no one played at all.
I climbed the stool and tried the keys, and soon I found a song.
And oh, I knew right then and there that here's where I belong.

As long as I can keep on playing, I'm happy as can be.
Everybody said the piano is broken, but it seems to play for me.

This old piano's got eighty-eight keys, and six of them don't play.
It's out of tune, but Honkytonk is better off that way.
Hey, the color is a dusty rose, and the whole front board is gone.
So you can watch all the hammers dance
as the music moves along.

As long as I can keep on playing, I'm happy as can be.
Some might say the piano is broken, but it seems to play for me.
Yeah, it plays like crazy for me.

LEAP TO PAGE 42
FOR MUSIC AND
FULL LYRICS!

Last week I bought me a cowboy hat. Now you guys are wearing them, too.
Why oh why do you Copycat, when I don't Copycat you?

SONG 7

༄ Copycat ༄

You're my three best friends and I like you a lot.
We have a good time, it's true. (IT'S TRUE!)
We go outside when it's cold or hot,
and we always find things to do. (TO DO!)
Yeah, my three best friends 'most every way.
I've got no doubt about that. (ABOUT THAT!)
But there is one thing I'd like to say:
I really don't like it when you Copycat.

(WHEN YOU COPYCAT!)

No, no, no!
Copycat. (COPYCAT!) Copycat. (COPYCAT!)
Please (PLEASE!) don't (DON'T!) Copycat.
Copycat. (COPYCAT!) Copycat. (COPYCAT!)
I really don't like it when you Copycat.
(I REALLY DON'T LIKE IT WHEN YOU COPYCAT!)

LEAP TO PAGE 44
FOR MUSIC AND
FULL LYRICS!

You and I share a love of weather. Come and sit beside me and we'll watch together.

End of a Summer Storm

It's easy to be happy on a sunny day,
but I often like it better when the day is gray.
Maybe it rains, and maybe you'll stay
here inside. Here with me.

You and I share a love of weather.
Come and sit beside me and we'll watch together.
Bright and brave, safe and warm,
as we wait for a summer storm.
Don't be afraid. Don't be afraid.

There's a rising wind and a falling rain,
beautiful patterns on the windowpane.
Fast and free, then it's quiet again
at the end of a summer storm.

LEAP TO PAGE 46
FOR MUSIC AND
FULL LYRICS!

You can recognize me by my rose-colored shades
as I make my strolling way through the Everglades.

SONG 9

Alligator Stroll

Well, I was born on a Friday in the Florida sun,
by the Kissimmee River, and before I was one,
my Mama Alligator said to me with a smile,
"Let me show you how to walk in a particular style.
*You take a little bit of Country and some slow Rock-and-Roll,
and what you've got going is the Alligator Stroll.*"

Okay.

I hold my head up high. I keep my feet on the ground.
I never hurry, never worry, as I'm strolling around.
I can keep a certain tempo that is lazy and sweet.
And I don't need shoes 'cause I've got alligator feet.
*Take a little bit of Country and some slow Rock-and-Roll,
and what you've got going is the Alligator Stroll.*

TURN THE PAGE TO LEARN
THE ALLIGATOR STROLL!
LEAP TO PAGE 47 FOR
MUSIC AND FULL LYRICS!

HERE'S HOW YOU DO
The Alligator Stroll

Put on your sunglasses. Form a line with the other Alligators. Now:

1. TAKE EIGHT SLOW STEPS FORWARD WITH A CLAP BETWEEN EACH STEP

LEFT [CLAP!] RIGHT [CLAP!] LEFT [CLAP!] RIGHT [CLAP!] LEFT [CLAP!] RIGHT [CLAP!] LEFT [CLAP!] RIGHT [CLAP!]
  1   2   3   4   1   2   3   4

2. TAKE THREE QUICK SIDEWAYS STEPS LEFT STILL FACING FORWARD

LEFT–RIGHT–LEFT [CLAP!]
   1   and   2

3. ROCK BACK ONTO YOUR RIGHT FOOT, FORWARD ONTO YOUR LEFT WITH A CLAP IN BETWEEN THE ROCKING

RIGHT [CLAP!] LEFT [CLAP!]
  3   4

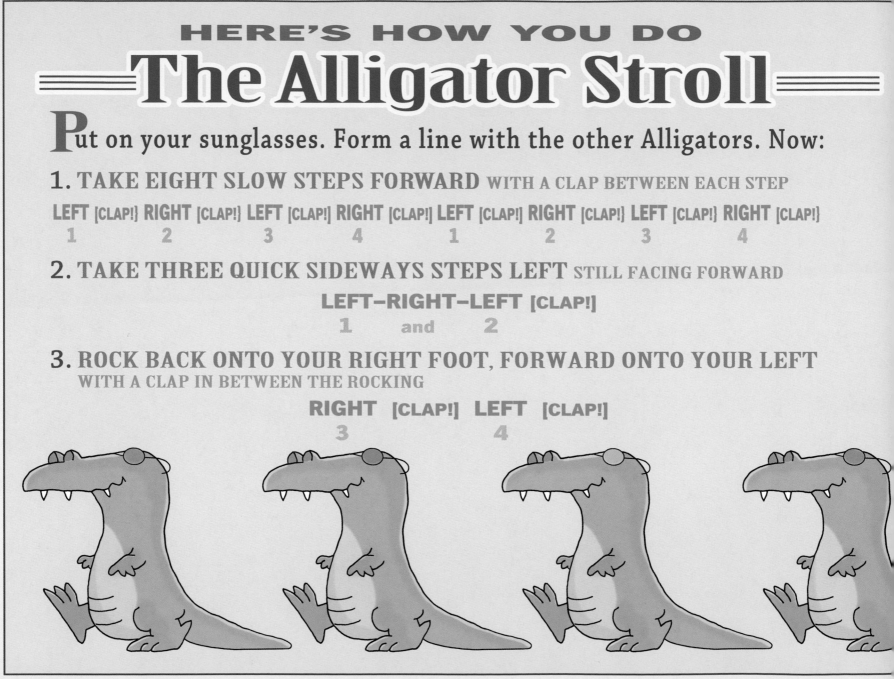

4. **TAKE THREE QUICK SIDEWAYS STEPS RIGHT** STILL FACING FORWARD

RIGHT–LEFT–RIGHT [CLAP!]

1   and   2

5. **ROCK BACK ONTO YOUR LEFT FOOT, FORWARD ONTO YOUR RIGHT** WITH A CLAP IN BETWEEN THE ROCKING

LEFT [CLAP!] **RIGHT** [CLAP!]

3   4

6. **TAKE FOUR SLOW STEPS FORWARD** WITH A CLAP BETWEEN EACH STEP

LEFT [CLAP!] **RIGHT** [CLAP!] **LEFT** [CLAP!] **RIGHT** [CLAP!]

1   2   3   4

7. **TAKE SEVEN QUICK STEPS TO TURN IN PLACE, IN A LITTLE CIRCLE** ALLIGATORS TURN LEFT, CHICKENS TURN RIGHT

LEFT–RIGHT–LEFT–RIGHT–LEFT–RIGHT–LEFT [CLAP!]

1   and   2   and   3   and   4

REPEAT!

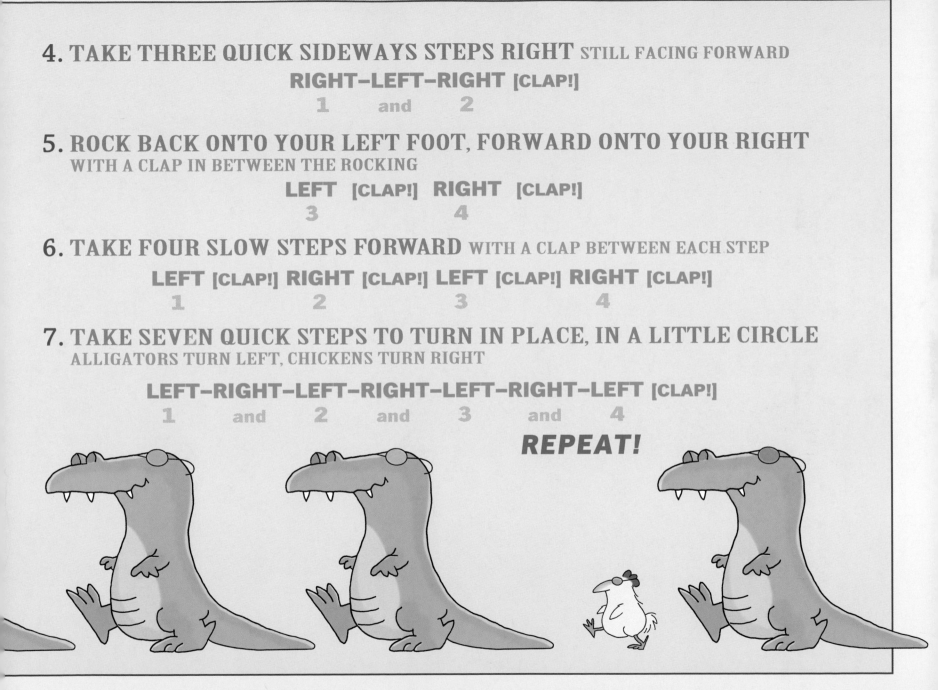

Beautiful Baby. Beautiful Child. Gentle and maybe just a little bit wild.

SONG 10

Beautiful Baby

Beautiful Baby. Beautiful Child.
Gentle and maybe just a little bit wild.
When I see your face, I know that it's true.
No one anyplace is beautiful as you.
Beautiful as you. Baby.

Beautiful Baby. Beautiful Child.
Gentle and maybe just a little bit wild.
When I hear you laugh, it's music and gold.
You bring to my life miracles untold. Baby.

And now you smile. I look in your eyes.
It's all worthwhile, and I realize
how beautiful. So beautiful. Simply beautiful.
Oh, Child. Child of mine. Hey, yeah.

LEAP TO PAGE 48 FOR MUSIC AND FULL LYRICS!

Deepest Blue. Hmm, Deepest Blue.

SONG
11

∽Deepest Blue ∾

I know—
 the color of the ocean.
 I know the color of the night.
 I know the color of a faraway song,
 and oh, it's always so right.
 Deepest Blue. Hmm, Deepest Blue.

The sky blue days of Summer,
 the golden afternoons of Fall,
 the soft silver twilight of Winter.
 Deepest Blue follows them all.

They say blue's the color of sadness.
 But sadness is only just gray.
 The deepest of blues lines the horizon
 when darkness fades into day.

LEAP TO PAGE 49
FOR MUSIC AND
FULL LYRICS!

Here we are, with the rest of our song!

SONG 12

More Frog Trouble

CHORUS OF EARNEST COWBOYS:

Here we are, with the rest of our song!
You're amazed that we're still going strong!
There's a wind from the West,
and it blows…

FROG TROUBLE!

LEAP TO PAGE 50 TO SEE THE MUSIC!

CHOOSING THE RIGHT

Good Names for Dogs

HANK
WILLIE
ROVER
TIPPY
FANG
CHESTER
AUTRY
JAKE
CODY
SHADOW
CHAOS
ANNIE
SPORT
MORGAN
SCOOTER
ELVIS
PATSY
BARKER

Good Names for Horses

SILVER
TRIGGER
CHAMPION
PAINT
SMOKE
DUSTY
SCOUT
MISTY
REBEL
STARDUST
LUCKY
FURY
LIGHTNING
BUCK
MIDNIGHT
FLASH
MAGIC
CIMARRON

NAME FOR YOUR PET!

Good Names for Alligators

Al

FLUFFY

VELVET

Good Names for Frogs

ERNEST
WILLIAM
FELICITY
HORATIO
PIERRE
BRIDGET
MAXWELL
ROSE
HENRY
CLEMENTINE
PRINCE
TENNESSEE
MAUDE
EUSTACE
CALAMITY
McKINLEY
PATIENCE
GREELY

PART TWO
SING AND PLAY ALONG

I'VE GOT A DOG

Lyrics & Music by Sandra Boynton

I've got a dog. And he's got me. We get a-long so eas-i-ly. Wher-ev-er I go, he's by my side. I've got a dog. I'm sat-is-fied. I've got a dog. He howls a-long when-ev-er I play a lone-some song. I've got a dog. I call him Hank. My luck-y stars I sure do thank. Well, he won't win a prize for be-ing dog - pret-ty at a fan-cy show in the great big cit-y. He's a mix of hound and I-don't-know-what. A hun-dred per - cent pure Junk - yard Mutt.

Oh, I've got a dog. He's really smart.
Got soulful eyes, and a big ol' heart.
This dog of mine, he doesn't bark.
Except all day, and after dark.

He's kind of proud. He won't do tricks.
My dog won't beg, or fetch me sticks.
He won't roll over if I say so.
If I say "Speak!" he just says "No."

Yeah, he won't win a prize for being dog-pretty
at a fancy show in the great big city.
He's a mix of hound and I-don't-know-what.
A hundred percent pure Junkyard Mutt.

I've got a dog. And he's got me. We get along so easily.
Wherever I go, he's by my side. I've got a dog. I'm satisfied.
I've got a dog. I'm satisfied. I've got a dog. I'm satisfied.
Come on, Hank!

TRUCKS

Lyrics by Sandra Boynton
Music by Sandra Boynton & Michael Ford

I'm sit-ting in this liv-ing room just play-ing my gui-tar. And now there comes a rum-bling sound from I don't know how far. I go right to the win-dow till she comes in-to view. There's no one no-where an-y-how loves trucks the way I do. *Get rolling.* [CHORUS] Big trucks and lit-tle trucks and long trucks and tall. Old trucks and new trucks, de-li-ver-y or long-haul. Sil-ver trucks and rust-y trucks and ev'-ry truck you see. As long as it's a truck, well it's just fine by me.

Downshift. Going uphill. Far back as I remember, it's always been this way. Whenever I see 'most any truck, it makes a better day. In every size and color, for anything you need, and oh, I like the music when they're shifting up to speed. *Skip-change it.* [CHORUS]

Throw it into fifth! There's nothing like a pickup truck for a winding dusty road. And you can't beat a trailer truck for any heavy load. And if I had a fire truck, then you could clang the bell. I'd be just fine with any truck, as anyone can tell. *Open it up.* [CHORUS]

One mile to go. I dream about the open road and traveling many days, and meeting many people with all their many ways. I dream about forgotten roads, and finding where they go. At night I'll sleep inside my truck, and this is what I know. *Bring it home.*
[CHORUS] As long as it's a truck, well it's just fine by me. As long as it's a truck, you know it's just fine by me.

FROG TROUBLE

Lyrics & Music by Sandra Boynton

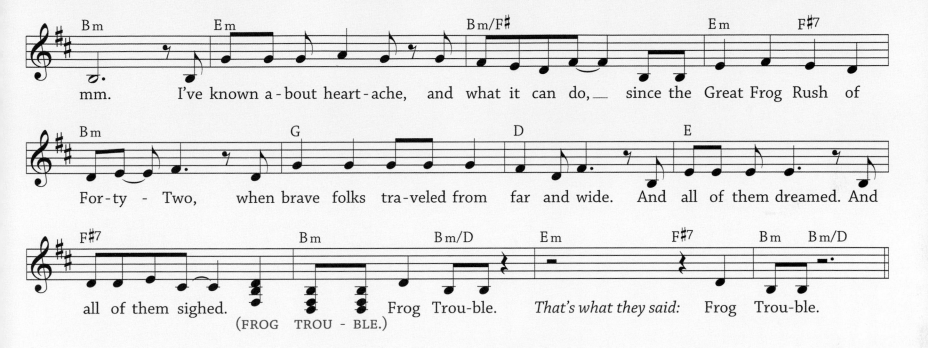

Now you seem confused by the things that I say.
What is this Frog Trouble, anyway?
Come a little closer and I'll tell you, my friend.
I don't know either. It's just pretend. Frog Trouble. *I made it all up. Yep.*

I have never met frogs face to faces. I don't know any frogs on a first name basis.
And it's hard to imagine what the trouble might be. But I like to say it importantly.
Frog Trouble.
Bad, bad Frog Trouble.

So you don't know me, and I don't know you. But I'm telling you this, and it might be true.
There's only one thing gets a Cowboy down. It's the kind of trouble that we've got in this town. Frog Trouble.
It's been pretty rough. (FROG TROUBLE.) *You've got to be tough.* Frog Trouble. *Oh, no. Just what I need.* (TROUBLE.)
Another frog stampede. Frog Trouble. (FROG TROUBLE.) Frog Trouble. (FROG TROUBLE.) Frog Trouble. Hmm-mm.

★ HEARTACHE SONG

Lyrics & Music by Sandra Boynton

THEY__ MAKE ME clean up my room. And put a-way my toys.__ When com-pan-y comes, I can't make a-ny noise. Oo-wuh uh-uh uh-oh! THEY SAY I must take a bath. But I've had one be-fore. I'm just so up-set. I can't take an-y more. DON'T THEY RE-MEM-BER all the heart-ache so deep when some-bo-dy tells__ you__ it's time now for sleep?

Oo-wuh uh-uh uh-oh!
PLEASE LET ME stay up too late.
I don't want to go to bed.
I'm not even tired. I just want to play instead.
Won't somebody listen to these feelings of mine?
Can anyone hear me, or do I have to WHIIIIINE?

I DON'T WANT
to clean up my room.
Don't want to put away my toys.
When company comes, I prefer making noise.
I don't want any bath. Oh, and I never did.
It's a difficult world when you're only a kid.

THANK YOU!
GOODNIGHT!

WHEN PIGS FLY

Lyrics by Sandra Boynton
Music by Sandra Boynton & Michael Ford

I know you for a dream-er, 'cause I've been a dream-er, too. You've got that far-a-way look in your search-ing eyes, and a heart that's stead-y and true. And I think I know what you're look-ing for in the end-less blue of the sky. You wait for the time When Pigs Fly. Did I hear some-bod-y tell you that dreams are noth-ing but air? Did I hear some-bod-y try to say i-ma-gin-a-tion will take you no-where? If an-y-one says it can't be done, that's the time to sim-ply re-ply: "It's a beaut-i-ful thing When Pigs Fly."

You never know when it will be, but they will surely come around. Flashes of pink, and flashes of gold, and a distant and joyful sound When Pigs Fly. I know you for a dreamer, 'cause I've been a dreamer, too. You've got that faraway look in your searching eyes, and a heart that's steady and true. Now we suddenly see a dozen or more sailing in the clear blue sky. The time has come When Pigs Fly. Yeah, it's a beautiful thing When Pigs Fly.

42

6 ★ BROKEN PIANO

Lyrics by Sandra Boynton
Music by Sandra Boynton & Michael Ford

I____ don't know just how old I was, but when I was quite small, I found an old pi-a-

- no that no one played at all.____ I climbed the stool and tried the keys, and

soon I____ found a song.____ And oh, I knew right then and there that here's where I be - long.

____ As long as I can keep on play-ing, I'm hap-py as can be.____ Ev'- ry - bo - dy said the pi -

a-no is bro-ken, but it seems to play for me.____ *Yeah.* This old pi-a-no's got

eight-y-eight keys and six of them don't play.____ It's out of tune, but Honk-y-tonk is bet-ter off that

way. Hey, the col-or is a dust-y rose, and the whole front board is gone.___ So

you can watch all the ham-mers dance as the mu-sic moves a-long.___ As long as I can

keep on play-ing, I'm hap-py as can be.___ Some might say the pi - a - no is bro - ken, but it

seems to play for me.___ Yeah, it plays like cra-zy for me.___

My Granddad listened to me play,
and he began to smile.
He played a fiddle tune for me.
We both played for a while.
And when I had to leave,
he said, "Come back
whenever you can."
And ever since,
'most every day, you'll
find me there again.
Here we go.

Yeah, Jukebox, Ragtime,
Honkytonk, Swing.
We have a good time
with everything.
As long as we can
keep on playing,
we're happy as can be.
Everybody said the
piano is broken,
but it plays for
him and me.

I don't know just how old I was,
but when I was quite small,
I found an old piano
that no one played at all.
The worn-out tag
inside the back says 1923.
Everybody said the
piano is broken
but it plays like crazy.
Plays like crazy.
Yeah, it plays like crazy for me.

7 COPYCAT

Lyrics & Music by Sandra Boynton

You're my three best friends and I like you a lot. We have a good time, it's true. (IT'S TRUE!) We go out-side when it's cold or hot, and we al-ways find things to do. (TO DO!) Yeah, my three best friends 'most ev-e-ry way. I've got no doubt a-bout that. (A-BOUT THAT!) But there is one thing I'd like to say: I real-ly don't like it when you Cop-y-cat. (WHEN YOU COP-Y-CAT!) No, no, no! Cop-y-cat. (COP-Y-CAT!) Cop-y-cat. (COP-Y-CAT!) Please (PLEASE!) don't (DON'T!) Cop-y-cat. Cop-y-cat. (COP-Y-CAT!) Cop-y-

cat. (COP - Y - CAT!)   I real - ly don't like it when you Cop - y - cat. (I

REAL - LY DON'T LIKE IT WHEN YOU COP - Y - CAT!) *That's so annoying.* (SO AN - NOY - ING.)

Last week I bought me a cowboy hat. Now you guys are wearing them, too. (WEARING THEM, TOO.)
Why oh why do you Copycat, when I don't Copycat you? (COPYCAT YOU.)
No, no, no! Copycat. (COPYCAT!) Copycat. (COPYCAT!) Please (PLEASE!) don't (DON'T!) Copycat.
Copycat. (COPYCAT!) Copycat. (COPYCAT!) I really don't like it when you Copycat. (I REALLY DON'T
LIKE IT WHEN YOU COPYCAT!) *Stop it.* (STOP IT!) *No, seriously.* (NO, SERIOUSLY.) *I mean it.* (I MEAN IT!)

Well, I know you think it's funny (IT'S FUNNY!) 'cause I can't get you to stop. (STOP!)
But I can make you be a copy bunny (OH BOY!) if I start going HOP (HOP) HOP (HOP) HOP (HOP) HOP (HOP)
HOP HOP HOP HOP HOP HOP HOP.

Now I have a new kitty called Maybellene, with pretty eyes of blue. (EYES OF BLUE!)
But she's not the only Maybellene I've ever seen. You each have a Maybellene, too. (MAYBELLENE, TOO!)
Yeah, one two three! Copycats. (COPYCATS!) Copycats. (COPYCATS!) Please (PLEASE!) don't (DON'T!) Copycat.
Copycat. (COPYCAT!) Copycat. (COPYCAT!) I really don't like it when you Copycat. (I REALLY DON'T LIKE IT WHEN YOU COPYCAT!)

You're my three best friends and I like you a lot. We have a good time, it's true. (IT'S TRUE!)
But if you want to Copycat, I'd really rather not, so I tell you what I'm gonna do. (GONNA DO!)
Ready? (READY?)

**I'M GONNA TALK TALK TALK JUST AS FAST AS I CAN DO IT KNOWING NOBODY CAN COPYCAT UNTIL I'VE GOTTEN THROUGH IT
AND IT DOESN'T REALLY MATTER WHETHER ANYTHING MAKES SENSE (YOU CAN ASK THE ALLIGATORS WHO ARE SLEEPING
ON THE FENCE) SO YOU MIGHT AS WELL GIVE UP AND GO TOBOGGANING INSTEAD BECAUSE THERE WASN'T ANY STOPPING
AND YOU DON'T KNOW WHAT I SAID.**
Copy that. (COPY THAT!) *Very funny.*

END OF A SUMMER STORM

Lyrics by Sandra Boynton
Music by Sandra Boynton & Michael Ford

It's ea-sy to be hap-py on a sun-ny day, but I of-ten like it bet-ter when the day is gray. May-be it rains, and may-be you'll stay here in-side. Here with me.

You and I__ share a love of wea-ther. Come and sit be-side me and we'll watch to-ge-ther.

Bright and brave, safe and warm, as we wait for a sum-mer storm. Don't be a-fraid. Don't be a-fraid.

There's a ris-ing wind and a fall-ing rain, beau-ti-ful pat-terns on the win-dow-pane.

Fast and free, then it's qui-et a-gain at the end of a sum-mer storm.

You and I share a love of weather. Now you are beside me and we watch together.
Bright and brave. Safe. Warm. At the end of a summer storm.
There's a rising wind and a falling rain, beautiful patterns on the windowpane.
Fast and free, then it's quiet again at the end of a summer storm.
At the end of a summer storm.

ALLIGATOR STROLL

Lyrics & Music by Sandra Boynton

Well, I was born on a Fri - day in the Flo - ri - da sun, by the Kis - sim - mee Ri - ver, and be - fore I was one,__ my Ma - ma Al - li - ga - tor said to me with a smile, "Let me show you how to walk in a par - ti - cu - lar style. You take a lit - tle bit of Coun - try and some slow Rock - and - Roll,__ and what you've got go - ing is the Al - li - ga - tor Stroll."__ *Okay*.

I hold my head up high. I keep my feet on the ground. I never hurry, never worry, as I'm strolling around.
I can keep a certain tempo that is lazy and sweet. And I don't need shoes 'cause I've got alligator feet.
Take a little bit of Country and some slow Rock-and-Roll, and what you've got going is the Alligator Stroll. I don't want to fight. I don't want to bite. I use my seventy-five teeth for a smile so bright. You can recognize me by my rose-colored shades as I make my strolling way through the Everglades. I'm strolling. Still strolling. *Yeah.* Oh whoa, bless my soul, what we've got going is the Alligator Stroll. *Left. Right. Left. Right.* I got a letter from my cousins in the Great Dismal Swamp. They said they want to teach me their Alligator Stomp. So I'm strolling that direction in the way that I do. I hope to reach the Carolinas by the time I'm 82. If you like a little Country and some slow Rock-and-Roll, you can follow right behind me with the Alligator Stroll. *Put on your shades. Looks good. Follow me.* We're going: Left. Right. Left. Right. Give a Hollywood smile with those teeth so white. Now stroll to the left. Back. Forth. Now we're strolling to the right. *Step South. Step North.* Now we're strolling straight ahead in an alligator row. And every now and then we do a little do-si-do. Hey, rock. Roll. Rock. Roll all the way to Carolina with the Alligator...*I'm in no hurry*...Stroll. *See you later. Alligator.*

10 BEAUTIFUL BABY

Lyrics & Music by Sandra Boynton

Beau-ti-ful Ba-by. Beau-ti-ful Child. Gen-tle and may-be just a lit-tle bit

wild. When I see your face, I know that it's true. No one an-y-place

is beau-ti-ful as you. Beau-ti-ful as you. Ba - by. Beau-ti-ful

Ba - by. Beau - ti - ful Child. Gen-tle and may-be

just a lit-tle bit wild. When I hear you laugh, it's mu-sic and gold.

You bring to my life mi-ra-cles un - told. Ba - by.

And now you smile. I look in your eyes. It's all worthwhile. And I realize how beautiful.
So beautiful. Simply beautiful. Oh, Child. Child of mine. Hey, yeah.
Beautiful Baby. Beautiful Child. Gentle and maybe just a little bit wild. When I see your face,
I know that it's true. There's no one anyplace as beautiful as you. Beautiful as you. Baby.

11 DEEPEST BLUE

Lyrics by Sandra Boynton
Music by Sandra Boynton & Michael Ford

I know the col-or of the o-cean. I know the col-or of the night. I know the col-or of a far-a-way song, and oh, it's al-ways so right. ___ Deep-est Blue. ___ Hmm, Deep-est Blue. The sky blue days of Sum-mer, the gold-en af-ter-noons of Fall, ___ the soft sil-ver twi-light of Win-ter. Deep-est Blue ___ fol-lows them all. They say blue's the col-or of sad - ness. But sad-ness is on-ly just gray. The deep-est of blues lines the hor-i-zon when dark-ness fades in-to day.

My love for you is the color of the ocean. My love for you is the color of the night.
My love for you is the color of forever. Deepest Blue, and forever all right.
Deepest Blue. Hmm, Deepest Blue. Oh, Deepest Blue. Blue. Deepest Blue. Ooo, hmmm.

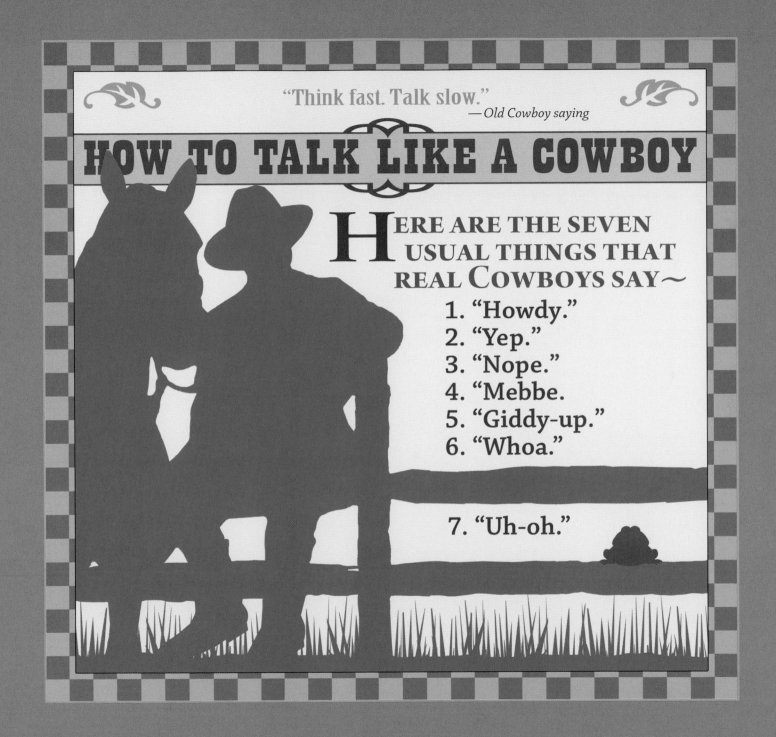

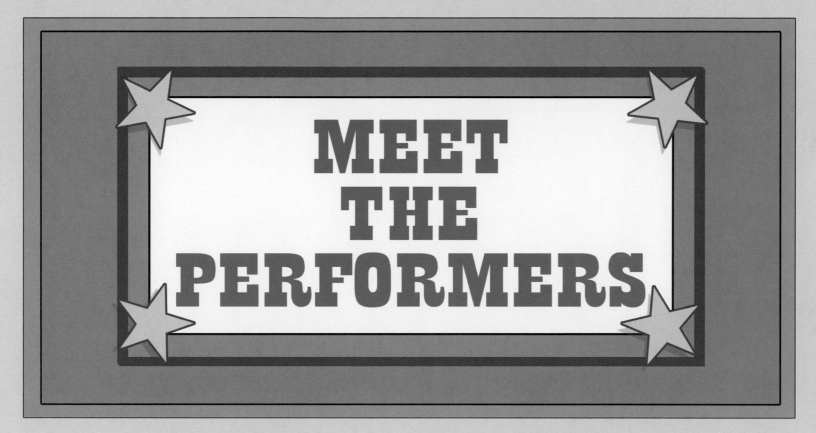

PART THREE

MEET
THE
PERFORMERS

Photographs and Biographies

The Singers and Bands in order of appearance

DWIGHT YOAKAM SINGS "I'VE GOT A DOG"

Maverick singer, guitar-slinger, songwriter, and movie actor. Sly, inventive traditionalist with a knowing way about him.

BEST KNOWN FOR
many great albums, and many chart singles, including "Guitars, Cadillacs" "Ain't That Lonely Yet" and "Fast As You"

photo: Randee St. Nicholas

BORN IN KENTUCKY, RAISED IN OHIO • NOW LIVES IN LOS ANGELES

BEST KNOWN FOR
chart singles "Stacy's Mom" and "Radiation Vibe," five classic studio albums, and one lone retro Country track, "Hung Up On You"

FOUNTAINS of WAYNE PERFORM "TRUCKS"

photo: Violeta Alvarez

BASED OUT OF NEW YORK CITY AND BEYOND

Iconic and revered rock band, noted for their smart songwriting and meticulous music production.

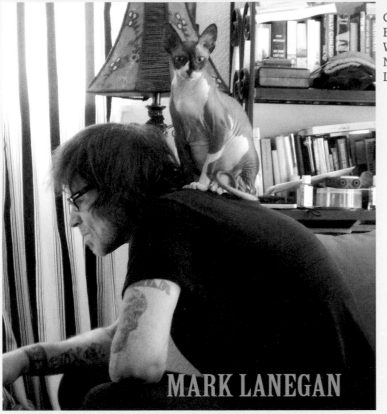

photo: Duke Garwood

photo: Duke Garwood

GREW UP IN ELLENSBURG, WASHINGTON • NOW LIVES IN LOS ANGELES

MARK LANEGAN

SINGS *"FROG TROUBLE"*

Soulful rocker, smoldering bluesman, and songwriter of gravity and light.

BEST KNOWN FOR

fronting the grunge band Screaming Trees, guesting with Queens of the Stone Age, brooding and beautiful solo albums, and exquisite collaborations with Isobel Campbell

KACEY MUSGRAVES

SINGS *"HEARTACHE SONG"*

Spirited young singer and guitarist with power and grace. Songwriter with style, originality, insight, and spark.

BEST KNOWN FOR

her poetic, understated single, "Merry Go 'Round"

photo: Kelly Christine

FROM GOLDEN, TEXAS • NOW LIVES IN NASHVILLE

photo: David Black

RYAN ADAMS

heartbreaking
quick
idealistic
uneasy
irreverent
chimerical

singer
guitar player
songwriter
producer
poet

SINGS "WHEN PIGS FLY"

FROM RALEIGH, NORTH CAROLINA •
NOW LIVES IN LOS ANGELES

BEST KNOWN FOR

fronting the band Whiskeytown, and thereafter for creating
so many glorious albums, including *Heartbreaker, Gold,*
and (with The Cardinals) *Jacksonville City Nights*

BEN FOLDS
*SINGS AND PLAYS
"BROKEN PIANO"*
lead vocal, upright piano

Exuberant, quirky,
and endlessly
inventive
songwriter,
singer,
piano player,
bandleader,
and record
producer.

BEST KNOWN FOR
superb albums
(solo and with
Ben Folds Five)
and great songs
including
"Philosophy"
"The Luckiest"
"Emaline"
and
"Erase Me"

GREW UP IN
WINSTON-SALEM,
NORTH CAROLINA •
NOW LIVES IN
NASHVILLE

photo: Autumn de Wilde

photo: Jim Shea

BRAD PAISLEY *SINGS AND PLAYS "COPYCAT"*

lead vocal, electric guitar

Way cool singer, blazing electric guitar player, and supremely clever songwriter.

BEST KNOWN FOR

many lively albums, and chart singles including
"Celebrity" "Then" "The World"
and "This Is Country Music"

FROM
GLEN DALE,
WEST VIRGINIA •
NOW LIVES IN
NASHVILLE

photo: Randee St. Nicholas

ALISON KRAUSS

SINGS "END OF A SUMMER STORM"

Ethereal singer, astonishing Bluegrass fiddle player, and meticulous record producer.

BEST KNOWN FOR

her long-time work with Union Station
and her gorgeous and melancholy
recordings including
"Endless Highway"
"Oh, Atlanta"
and "The Lucky One"

GREW UP IN CHAMPAIGN, ILLINOIS • NOW LIVES IN NASHVILLE

Photo: George Holz

JOSH TURNER

SINGS "ALLIGATOR STROLL"

Honey-voiced singer and songwriter of deep sincerity and easygoing charm.

BEST KNOWN FOR

his heartfelt albums and chart singles, including "Long Black Train" "Would You Go With Me?" and "Why Don't We Just Dance"

GREW UP IN HANNAH, SOUTH CAROLINA •
NOW LIVES IN NASHVILLE

DARIUS RUCKER

SINGS "BEAUTIFUL BABY"

Likable, powerful frontman and songwriter for the rock band Hootie & the Blowfish, now turned Country star.

courtesy CMA Music Fest

BORN IN CHARLESTON, SOUTH CAROLINA, AND HAS LIVED THERE ALL HIS LIFE

BEST KNOWN FOR

Hootie & the Blowfish chart singles "Let Her Cry" and "Hold My Hand"

Three bestselling solo Country albums, with chart singles including "Don't Think I Don't Think About It" "Come Back Song" and "This"

photo: Carolina Palmgren

GREW UP IN BRAINERD, MINNESOTA • NOW LIVES NEAR NEW YORK CITY

LINDA EDER *SINGS "DEEPEST BLUE"*

Glorious, renowned singer and stage actress, who moves easily across diverse styles—Broadway, blues, jazz, pop, old standards, and Country.

BEST KNOWN FOR

many albums, many sold-out concerts around the world, and her award-winning starring role in the Broadway musical *Jekyll & Hyde*

FALLS MOUNTAIN COWBOYS

PERFORM "MORE FROG TROUBLE"
(AND ALSO THE OVERTURE TO "FROG TROUBLE")

All four harmonizing Cowboys were previously members of The Uninvited Loud Precision Band, an equally sincere and nonexistent ensemble. They chose this line of work because they like to sing and they look good in hats.

MIKE FORD baritone GRAHAM STONE lead tenor
DEVIN MCEWAN bass KEITH BOYNTON baritone

photo: Jonathan Doster

BORN AND BRED HERE AND THERE

The Musicians

STUART DUNCAN
FIDDLE, MANDOLIN

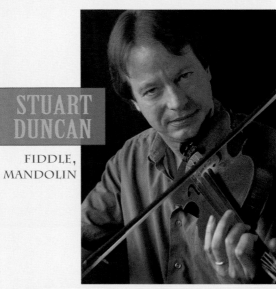

SAN DIEGO, CALIFORNIA • NOW FROM NASHVILLE

RON BLOCK
BANJO, ACOUSTIC GUITAR

photo: Alex Blagg

INGLEWOOD, CALIFORNIA • NOW FROM NASHVILLE

MICHAEL FORD
PIANO, KEYBOARDS

PHILADELPHIA, PENNSYLVANIA •
NOW FROM NOWHERE, CONNECTICUT

photo: Beth Andrien

SHANNON FORREST
DRUMS

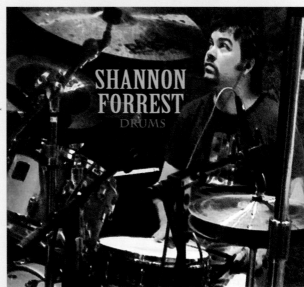

EASLEY, SOUTH CAROLINA • NOW FROM NASHVILLE

THE SCOTTY BROTHERS
SPOONS

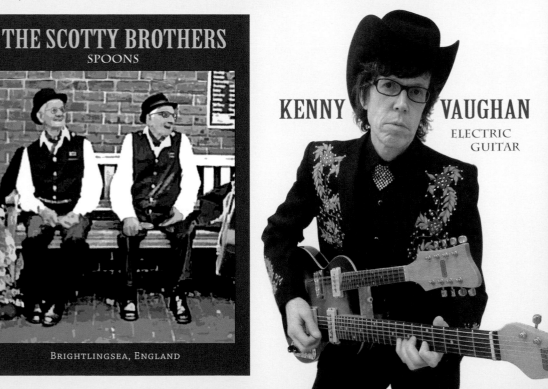

BRIGHTLINGSEA, ENGLAND

KENNY VAUGHAN
ELECTRIC GUITAR

DENVER, COLORADO • NOW FROM NASHVILLE

photo: Jeff Bender

VIKTOR KRAUSS
UPRIGHT BASS

CHAMPAIGN, ILLINOIS • NOW FROM NASHVILLE

JIM HOKE   HARMONICA, SAXOPHONE

SCHENECTADY, NEW YORK • NOW FROM NASHVILLE

photo: Lisa Haddad

RUSS PAHL

photo: Michael Wilson

PEDAL STEEL

MINNEAPOLIS, MINNESOTA • NOW FROM NASHVILLE

GRANTS PASS, OREGON • NOW FROM NASHVILLE

photo: Joel Micah Dennis

LUKE BULLA
FIDDLE

photo: Gordon White

BRYAN OWINGS
DRUMS
COLUMBUS, MISSISSIPPI • NOW FROM NASHVILLE

PITTSBURGH, PENNSYLVANIA • NOW FROM NASHVILLE

ROY AGEE
TROMBONE

DEAN PARKS

BANJO, ACOUSTIC GUITAR

FORT WORTH, TEXAS • NOW FROM LOS ANGELES

RECORDING CREDITS

All recording sessions produced by Sandra Boynton • All tracks arranged and mixed by Boynton and Michael Ford at Studio Mike (Connecticut), Blackbird Studios (Nashville), and The Studio (Portland, Maine) • Viktor Krauss, session leader and music advisor

I've Got a Dog **Dwight Yoakam, lead vocal**

VOCAL RECORDED AT Henson Studios, Los Angeles
ENGINEER Marc DeSisto ASSISTANT Kevin Mills
BAND Kenny Vaughan, Stuart Duncan, Russ Pahl,
Michael Ford, Ron Block, Viktor Krauss
DOG (BARK-UP SINGER) Keith Boynton

Trucks **Fountains of Wayne**

BAND Chris Collingwood, Adam Schlesinger,
Jody Porter, Brian Young
RECORDED AT Stratosphere Sound, New York City
ENGINEER Geoff Sanoff
MORE BAND Stuart Duncan, Dean Parks, Ron Block
Track co-produced with Fountains of Wayne

Frog Trouble **Mark Lanegan, lead vocal**

VOCAL RECORDED AT Ben's Studio, Nashville
ENGINEER Leslie Richter ASSISTANT Sorrel Brigman
BAND Kenny Vaughan, Ron Block, Dean Parks,
Jim Hoke, Michael Ford, Russ Pahl
COWBOY CHORUS Falls Mountain Cowboys

Heartache Song **Kacey Musgraves, lead vocal**

VOCAL RECORDED AT Ben's Studio, Nashville
ENGINEER Leslie Richter
BAND Kenny Vaughan, Jim Hoke, Michael Ford
HIGH HARMONIES Beth Andrien Ford

When Pigs Fly **Ryan Adams, lead vocal**

VOCAL RECORDED AT PaxAm Studio, Los Angeles
ENGINEER David LaBrel
BAND Ron Block, Michael Ford, Stuart Duncan, Viktor Krauss

Broken Piano **Ben Folds, lead vocal & piano**

VOCAL & PIANO RECORDED AT Ben's Studio, Nashville
ENGINEER Joe Costa ASSISTANT Leslie Richter
BAND Stuart Duncan, Viktor Krauss, Michael Ford

Album mastered by
BOB LUDWIG
GATEWAY MASTERING
PORTLAND, MAINE
(tracks 3 and 12 Frog Trouble Theme
mastered by Robert C. Ludwig)

Sound effects used under license:
track 2 VROOM/audiosparx.com
track 3 STAMPEDE/sfxsource.com
track 3 & 12 RIBBIT & WHINNY #2/sounddogs.com

Copycat **Brad Paisley, lead vocal & electric guitar**

VOCAL & LEAD GUITAR RECORDED AT The Farm, Nashville
ENGINEER Neal Cappellino HARMONIES Fountains of Wayne
BAND Kenny Vaughan, Stuart Duncan, Ron Block,
Viktor Krauss, Michael Ford, Russ Pahl, Shannon Forrest

End of a Summer Storm **Alison Krauss, lead vocal**

VOCAL RECORDED AT The Doghouse, Nashville
ENGINEER Neal Cappellino BAND Ron Block, Michael Ford,
Roy Agee, Viktor Krauss *Track co-produced with Viktor Krauss*

Alligator Stroll **Josh Turner, lead vocal**

VOCAL RECORDED AT The Doghouse, Nashville
ENGINEER Neal Cappellino
BAND Michael Ford, Kenny Vaughan,
Shannon Forrest, Bryan Owings, Viktor Krauss

Beautiful Baby **Darius Rucker, lead vocal**

VOCAL RECORDED AT The Doghouse, Nashville
ENGINEER Neal Cappellino
BAND Dean Parks, Michael Ford

Deepest Blue **Linda Eder, lead vocal**

VOCAL RECORDED AT Studio Mike, Connecticut
ENGINEER Michael Ford
BAND Michael Ford, Kenny Vaughan, Jim Hoke,
Luke Bulla, Bryan Owings, Viktor Krauss

More Frog Trouble **Falls Mountain Cowboys**

VOCALS RECORDED AT Studio Mike, Connecticut ENGINEER Michael Ford
BAND Ron Block, Kenny Vaughan, and the Michael Ford Orchestra
WHINNY #1 by kind permission of HORSE PRESENCE, PACIFICA, CA horsepresence.com
WHIPSNAP by Adam Winrich, by kind permission of VOLUME ONE, EAU CLAIRE, WISCONSIN

THE SPOONS ON "I'VE GOT A DOG" ARE PERFORMED BY PETER AND GORDON SCOTT OF ENGLAND, IN A SONG CALLED "JAM FOR A SPOON" BY TIM WHEELER. USED BY KIND PERMISSION OF TIM WHEELER AND PETER SCOTT. TO WATCH THE TERRIFIC VIDEO, SEARCH YOUTUBE FOR "THE AMAZING SCOTTY BROTHERS."

Instruments for all tracks (other than "Trucks") recorded at House of Blues, Nashville RECORDING ENGINEER Neal Cappellino ASSISTANT Chris Wilkinson
Additional tracking for "Alligator Stroll" and "Deepest Blue" done at Ben's Studio, Nashville RECORDING ENGINEER Joe Costa ASSISTANT Leslie Richter
Dean Parks self-recorded his guitar in his Los Angeles studio • Michael Ford self-recorded his keyboards in his Connecticut studio

BOOK CREDITS & THANK-Y'ALLS

EDITOR **Suzanne Rafer**
FEARLESS LEADER **Peter Workman**
VOICE OF REASON **Walter Weintz**
PRE-PRESS **Terry Ortolani**
FILE PREP **Bob Alessi**
MUSIC ENGRAVING **Bruce Johnson**
PRODUCTION **Doug Wolff**

ALWAYS THERE TO HELP
Jenny Mandel, Page Edmunds
Kim Hicks, Erin Klabunde
Deborah McGovern
Carol White
Phil Conigliaro
Carson Ortolani

SESSION VIDEOGRAPHY
Beth Andrien Ford

GREAT DEMO SINGERS
Michael Ford
Graham Stone
Beth Andrien Ford
Caitlin McEwan
Darcy Boynton

GOLDEN MUSICIAN AND FRIEND
Viktor Krauss

FABULOUS FAMILY AND FRIENDS
Jamie, Caty, Keith, Devin, Darcy
Beth, Rachel, John, Katie
Pam, John, Em, Robb
Laurie, Carl, Kyle, Marissa
Ash, Shaun, Henry, Carys
Jackie, Linda, Dara, Fred
Al, Suzanne, Nina • Laura and Marc
Sarah, Steve and Randy, Susan
Capecelatros, Rivkins
Kirbers, Clarkes, Manns
Ortolanis, Stanleys, Gummers

VERY THOUGHTFUL FOLKS
Tim Wheeler
Kristi Krauss
Kim Williams-Paisley
Jamie Kitman
Kendal Marcy
Sam Kapala, Don Mitchell
Sharon Corbitt-House, Jesse Scott
Warner Music Nashville
Cracker Barrel
Puckett's Grocery Store
Miel Restaurant
The Country Music Hall of Fame

BRILLIANT A and R
Christine Gray
Sarah Calhoun
Suzanne Rafer
Danny Peary
Robin Corey
Darcy Boynton
Devin McEwan
Jamie McEwan

PERFECTLY TIMED INSPIRATION
David Wykoff
Mark Robinson
Chandler Kinchla
Cynthia Weil

Thank you to every single one of the astonishingly great editorial, art, production, publicity, marketing, sales, and administration people at the incomparable Workman Publishing.

Adam Winrich
Andy Forward
Nick Meyer

ARTIST MANAGEMENT
Renee Behrman
Michael Corcoran
Hannah Cornforth
Jonathan Daniel
Lindsey Farwell
Kevin Gasser
David Hart
Justin Hinote
Jon Lullo
Laura McCorkindale
Scott McGhee
Michael Meisel
Erik Peterson
Kathleen Rabas
Todd Ramey
Kristy Reeves
Bill Simmons
Debbie Tirone
Alan Wolmark

MAKE A FOLDED-PAPER FROG PUPPET

WITH A REALLY BIG MOUTH

TROUBLE!

THIS IS TOO HARD!

YOU WILL NEED:

SCISSORS • DOUBLE-SIDED TAPE • LETTER-SIZE GREEN PAPER
2 BIG ROUND WHITE STICKERS • 2 SMALL ROUND BLACK STICKERS

To make your first frog, you can cut off the facing page!

1 To make a square from a rectangular piece of paper, fold one corner to its diagonal opposite. Cut off the extra paper. Your square now is a triangle.

fold

cut

2 Fold the two opposite ends of the triangle together. Now you have a smaller triangle.

fold

3 Open your paper back up so it's a square again. Then fold each corner to the center. It's now a smaller square.

4 Turn your square over. Then fold each new corner to the center. Now you have a small thick square.

5 Fold the square in half.

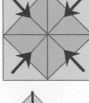

Now unfold it, and fold it the other way. Then unfold it.

6 Put your fingers inside the four sections. Tug on each of the four corners to make a diamond shape.

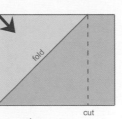

7 Using double-sided tape, attach the two top sections together. Then attach the bottom pair together. You can now move both parts,   like opening a mouth.

8 Stick the small black stickers on to the big white stickers. Frog eyes! Place them in the top two triangles. Then fold the two top corners backward.

And there you have it—

A FROG!

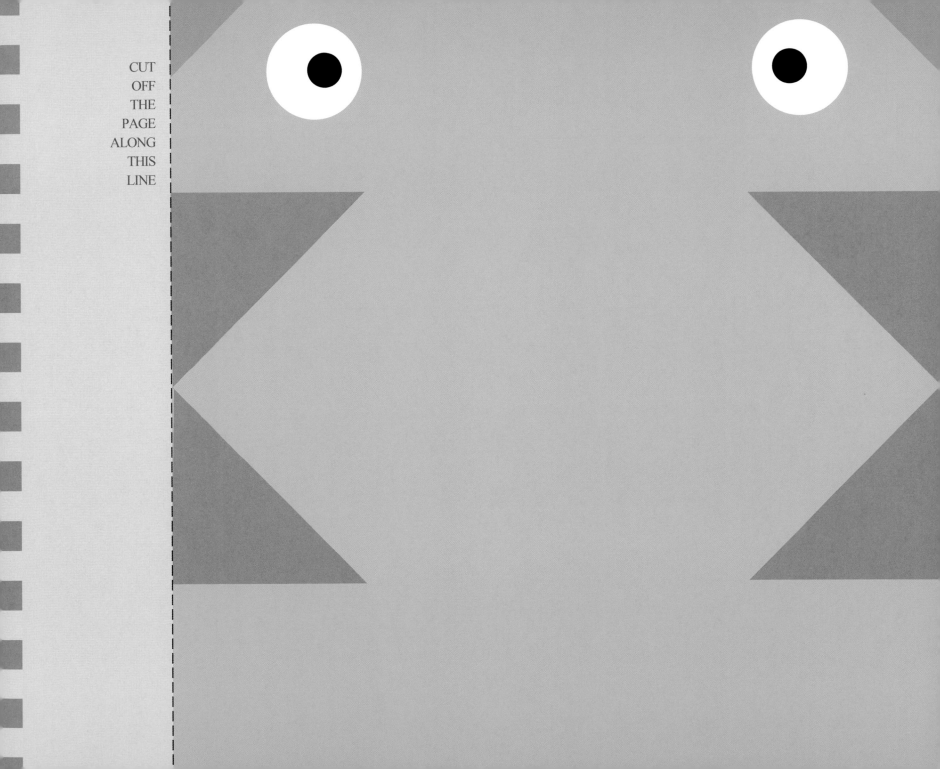

CUT
OFF
THE
PAGE
ALONG
THIS
LINE